DANCING FOR HIM (ON STAGE #1)

AN M/M ROMANCE

JEFF ADAMS

BIG GAY
Media

DANCING *for* HIM

JEFF ADAMS

DANCING FOR HIM (ON STAGE #1)

It takes two to tango… or waltz.

Hollywood electrician Todd Stewart is thrilled when he gets the opportunity to work on his favorite show, America's Next Top Dancer. What he doesn't expect is making a connection with Nathaniel Mayer, a contestant on the show and a dancer he's got a major crush on.

In creating a partnership that works, they must navigate the challenges of crazy schedules, fame and post-show commitments. Todd and Nate are determined to keep their run going long past the season finale.

Dancing for Him is book one in the *On Stage* series.

2nd edition, 2015 from Big Gay Media
1st edition, 2010 from Dreamspinner Press
Dancing for Him was originally published in 2010 under the title
Dancer & Sexy Big Man. This revised and expanded edition includes
scenes that did not appear in the original.

ISBN: 9780986136023

ONE

THE RINGING PHONE cut through my deep sleep. I was nestled under the covers and about as comfortable as possible. I braced for the worst as I fumbled around on the nightstand for my phone that seemed to be hiding from me.

"Hello?" I mumbled.

"Hey, Todd. It's Martin."

A grunt was all I could manage in response.

Martin was a good friend and colleague. We worked as electricians for Haphazard Productions. If he was calling, I needed to focus. I glanced at the clock and saw that it was a little after three in the morning. Luckily, I found the light switch on the first try. Illuminating the room helped me wake up.

"Hey. Yeah. What's up?" I finally asked.

"Sorry to call you so early. An opportunity came up I thought you might want."

I sat up. My eyes worked to adjust to the light. My brain, meanwhile, wanted none of it.

"Okay," I said, sounding groggy.

"One of the senior techs on *Top Dancer* had to go to Texas for a family emergency. They need someone... this morning. I said you might be available since you're on a hiatus."

"Oh. Yes. I'm interested. When?" Now I was awake. This was worth losing sleep over.

"Call's at five."

"I'll be there." I got up while still getting information from Martin.

There was no going back to sleep now. If they needed me on set at five, I'd need to be there by four-thirty to check in since I'd be the new guy. I got the bed made and headed to my galley-style kitchen to make coffee. I'd only gone to bed three hours ago, so there was going to be a lot of coffee today.

I was all too happy to give up part of an unexpected vacation to work on *America's Next Top Dancer*. I'd been off work for two days. The crew of *Dealmakers* found out on Monday that we were shut down for six to eight weeks because the host broke his arm in a weekend rock climbing accident. We had enough shows in the can that we could stop production, let him heal, and then resume shooting. The viewers would never see him in a cast.

ANTD was shot on the same studio lot as *Dealmakers*. When *ANTD* started three years ago I wanted to work on it, but I didn't have enough seniority to request the transfer. Even if this lasted only a few days, I was psyched to be a part of it.

I was a huge fan of the show, so much so that I made sure to watch it the same night it aired so I could vote. The current season, only four weeks into the ten-week competition, was one of the best yet. Nathaniel Mayer, a hot guy and an amazing dancer, was captivating. He got my votes every week. Now I'd see him dance in person. I was practically bouncing around the kitchen in excitement.

Seeing the dancers work, not just Nathaniel, was going to be awesome. I'd have to make sure to keep my focus on my duties, of course, but there'd be downtime when I could watch rehearsals and see what they did first hand.

I'd been into dance for years. I'd seen all kinds of great dancing at shows around L.A. I've set my TiVo to record anything with a dance theme. Sometimes I get crap, but sometimes I get stuff like the Alvin Ailey performance that aired on PBS a few nights ago.

I think my dad's the reason I got hooked on it. He's an electrician and I apprenticed with him on Broadway. We worked together on a couple of musicals and the dancing blew me away. We did a stint at New York's City Center for their fall dance festival and it was incredible seeing so many different kinds of dance on the stage.

I'd been tempted a time or two to take dance lessons. That seemed silly, though. Truthfully, I've got no rhythm. I'm a big guy, too, and I'm pretty sure my body isn't built to move like a dancer.

Yeah, I've seen the football players dance on the celebrity dancing show, but they already knew how to move because of the sport they played. Other than working out, I haven't been sporty since I graduated high school a decade ago.

The coffee finally finished dripping into the mug. I took it and headed off to the bathroom to grab a shower. I was never one to be late, but to work on *ANTD* there was no way I was going to be anything but punctual.

TWO

Jordan Seller, *ANTD's* lead technician, met me when I showed up at the production office. The office was a cramped space with more desks in the room than there should've been. Even at this hour, everyone seemed perky. No doubt the techno music playing in the background helped keep the mood up.

"Thanks for coming in," Jordan said. "Sorry we had Martin wake you in the middle of the night but we've got a lot of stuff to prep for this afternoon's results show."

"Not a problem. I'm happy to be here."

"Great. Here's your access pass. Are you available for the next week? We don't know the needs for next week's show yet, but given what we've done so far this season, I'm sure we can use you."

"Sure, *Dealmakers* is off for at least the next month."

"Perfect. Head over to stage twenty-three. Check

in with Clive Patterson. Anyone who's there can point him out. Thanks again, Todd." We shook hands and Jordan turned his attention to his computer.

Walking into stage twenty-three was a huge rush. I'd been around studios and celebrities for a few years, but this was a thrill for me. Even though I worked on the same lot, I'd never been inside since the shooting schedule for *America's Next Top Dancer* conflicted with *Dealmakers*.

The crew was already hard at work. From where I stood, just inside the entrance, I could see more than a dozen people throughout the soundstage. The lighting team was working on the grid, over the stage, refocusing lights while someone stood on the stage to mark the spot the lights needed to hit. At the back of the set, riggers prepared backdrops and worked with the technicians who programmed the big video screen along the back wall.

The cavernous building was dominated by the main stage. In front of the stage was a pit area where audience members could stand close to the action. Behind that were sections of bleacher seating for the rest of the audience. The judges' desk, on the left side of the stage, was disassembled. Everything was lit up with the show's typical color palette of blues highlighted with some red, green and orange. I assumed there was a good deal of space behind the stage too, considering the size of the props I'd seen them use.

I needed to stop ogling and get to work.

"Excuse me," I said to the next person that walked

by. The woman, who was carrying three binders and moving at a rapid pace, stopped and looked annoyed. "I'm looking for Clive Patterson. I'm the electric sub."

I guessed that was important to her because she immediately went from bothered to helpful. "Oh hey, great. He's going to be thrilled to see you," she said while her eyes darted around the studio. "There he is."

She pointed to an average-looking guy dressed in jeans and a black t-shirt who seemed to be fighting with electrical cords coming out of the front of the stage.

"Thanks." She was gone before I finished saying it.

I walked quickly to where Clive was and introduced myself. "Can I help you out with that?"

"For the love of God, yes! See those two grips?" he said as he gestured with his head, not letting go of the wires he held. "Pull that panel out, get under the stage and see what these are hung up on so I can get them out."

I removed the section of stage and climbed in. It was an uncomfortable place. I had to keep my six-two frame hunched over and dodge all the conduits and supports that were in place. I followed the cables to where the problem was and quickly untangled them so Clive could pull them out.

"Fantastic," he said. As soon as I was out from under the stage he came over to me, cables still in hand. "Thanks for coming in. Let's get you right into it. When we lit up the desk this morning, three-fourths of it failed, along with all the video monitors. I had somebody look at it first thing, but had to reassign her to help with the musical guest. They're in at noon for blocking and it's gonna be tight getting ready for them. Can you dive in with the desk?"

"Sure can. Where's your electric closet and supply area?"

"Closet is back by the crew door where you came in. Supplies are mostly in cabinets up top to keep them out of the way. As soon as I can spare someone, I'll have them give you a quick tour. Did you bring your radio?"

"Yes."

"Great. We're on channel twenty-three. If you need help, call out to me and I'll send someone. Otherwise, let me know when the desk is fixed."

"Sounds good. I'll get to it."

Clive clearly didn't have time for small talk, so I went up the access stairs to the desk and got to work.

I'd been there only five minutes, but I loved all the activity. Nothing much happens on *Dealmakers*. We usually reconfigure the set a bit at the start of the season and after that it's weeks of taping and routine maintenance. Here, it was a whirlwind.

The desk took about an hour to fix. Someone had spilled soda, and the sticky mess caused the electronics to short out. After that I helped set up for the guest artist. For the performance a platform had to be installed over the regular stage and it had to be electrified for lights and effects.

Clive had a great crew. They made it easy for me to

fall into step with them. We accomplished the major setup on time. While the singer did a sound check and camera blocking with her band and dancers, we grabbed lunch. After that, it was time for final checks to be ready for the audience to enter at three-thirty.

At five the live broadcast of the week's results show began for the East Coast. I watched from the grid, where I had to be to do my part when the singer's stage was put in place during a commercial break.

It was cool watching the show from above. I knew I'd watch again on TiVo later to see the dances from the right perspective, but the aerial view was pretty awesome. To be just thirty feet away from Nathaniel while he performed was the highlight of the day.

The show went off at six and once the audience was gone, we spent another hour shutting down.

"You did a great job today," Clive said as he shook my hand. "Thanks very much."

"Glad I could help."

"Tomorrow is our day off and then we're back on Friday to start setup for next Tuesday. I know you usually run Monday through Friday, but if we could get you for six days of Friday through Wednesday that would be great."

"No problem. Five on Friday?"

"We don't shoot that day, so make it eight. I'll make sure Melinda puts you on the call list emails so you get all the updates."

"Great. I'll see you then."

THREE

Friday was, shockingly, busier than Wednesday. Half the dances for the next show required things to be built and ready to install before the dancers moved from rehearsal studio to stage on Sunday. An incredible amount of work got done to prepare a dozen new scenic elements.

I finished the day putting things away up in the catwalks above the stage. Music started down on the stage, but not from the studio sound system. The song was the instrumental part from *A Chorus Line*'s "The Music and the Mirror." I looked down and saw Nathaniel at center stage.

As quietly as possible, I made my way to stage level. Nathaniel leapt through the air with his legs at full extension and his arms outstretched. It was incredible. Instant goosebumps. I stayed in the wings stage right and watched. He worked to create the perfect solo—thirty seconds that showed why he deserved the audience's votes.

As he worked, the routine got more complex, more graceful, more ... perfect. Watching his creative process intrigued me—he'd start, stop, reconsider, try things a few times, keep some moves and discard others. The routine closed with a leap in the air, landing on his left foot and then a drop down to his knees as he curled into a ball.

I clapped. I hadn't meant to. It was an involuntary reaction to a great performance. Unfortunately I scared him. He jumped and turned to look in my direction.

"Sorry, man. Didn't mean to startle you."

His smile was shy, like a kid who figured out he wasn't about to get in trouble. He went to the front of the stage and turned off the music, which had restarted, before coming over to me in the wings.

"'S okay. Didn't realize I had an audience. Crew guys don't usually pay attention to us. I'm Nathaniel... well Nate, really," he said, extending a hand for me to shake. "The producers insisted on the Nathaniel thing."

I was surprised at the firmness of his grip. I don't know why I didn't expect that from someone who was clearly so athletic, but it caught me off guard.

"Yeah. I've voted for you," I said, kicking myself for suddenly sounding like such a groupie. "I'm Todd."

His grin widened, more like the happy guy I'd seen on TV. "Cool, a fan. But I thought crew couldn't vote?"

"True. I'm filling in for a few days so I won't be able to vote this week."

"I'll have to get those votes from somewhere else, then." He winked at me as he wiped sweat off his forehead with the back of his hand. "So you liked the solo?"

I couldn't believe I was talking to Nathaniel... Nate. I had this season's shows saved on TiVo because I couldn't get enough of him. He was incredibly hot, even though he wasn't my usual type. Typically I go for guys like me—big, muscled, hairy, a good-looking bear. I like a guy you can grab onto and know he's not going to break. Nate, who was probably five-nine or five-ten, had a dancer's body—lean with well-defined muscles. His look, and the way he carried himself, caught my attention from the moment his audition aired.

His hazel eyes were enthralling. There were many shades of color in his irises. You couldn't see that on TV and I found it was difficult not to stare. The eyes, meanwhile, contrasted perfectly with his floppy black hair. It was hair you wanted to run your hand through.

"Yeah. I think it's your best yet. The way you did so many variations on jumps across the back of the stage, one after the other, and then the way you landed at the end... it was incredible. Good music choice, too."

"Thanks. Hopefully the home audience will like it."

I hadn't thought about that. I might've just seen a dance few others would see. So far, Nathaniel hadn't been in the bottom three so he wasn't performing solos. I already wanted to see it again.

I also wanted to touch him, run my hands over his taut body. He sported just a little bit of scruff around his chin and on his cheeks. I couldn't imagine he'd be able to grow a full beard, or even a goatee from the looks of it, but the stubble looked good on him. I already knew, from a shirtless dance he' done two weeks ago, that he was smooth except for a bit of a treasure trail.

"They're crazy if they put you in the bottom three to make you do it in the first place," I said, holding his gaze, probably longer than I should've. It wasn't uncomfortable; quite the opposite, actually. I would've been happy to stay with him all night just talking. "You should finish up. They're going to kick you out soon to lock up."

"Right. Have a good night, Todd."

"You, too."

Surprisingly he ran his hand down my shoulder and arm and gave me an *aw shucks* kind of smile before he walked away.

The guy totally felt me up.

It wasn't the touch of someone just saying goodbye, he gripped me several times as his hand traveled down my arm. His touch moved through me like an energy bolt.

He started the music and ran the routine again. I pulled myself away from the side of the stage and went to sign out for the night.

What would it be like to be with him? I imagined

what his flexible, agile body would be able to do. Was he even gay? I'd thought so from watching him on TV. He'd never said anything in any of the interview packages, but I got the vibe nonetheless. And he sure seemed flirtatious tonight.

FOUR

Saturday, Sunday and Monday went by in a blur. I understood now why this show had the reputation for being one of the busiest on the lot. Even though I watched, I didn't realize how little time the crew had to build out each week's production requirements. I had a great time in this environment. Every day brought a new challenge.

I found out on Sunday I would be with the show for a couple more weeks, at least. The guy I replaced needed some extended time for family matters. I felt bad for him, but I was psyched to hang around *ANTD* a little longer.

Nate and I were talking a couple times a day, which made me giddy. I never saw him, or any of the other dancers, talking to the tech crew unless it was directly related to a performance. So we had something going on, even if it was just the beginnings of a friendship.

We talked a lot about dance. I'd seen enough that I could speak somewhat intelligently about different styles. He was great and didn't get too technical with me. Like me, Nate got the love of what he did from his father, who'd been a pro ballroom dancer until a knee injury took him out of competition and moved him to teaching.

After all the strenuous prep work, Tuesday's performance show was easy for me. I was positioned stage left, at the end of the walkway. We had one special set up that was moved on and off the stage from there. I stood watch over it to be ready to place it on stage and connect it to the electric grid. I also made sure the audience didn't try to mess with it. I liked the position because it meant I got to watch the show from the audience's point of view.

All of the dancers did great. Nate did the solo I'd seen him working on since the producers decided it was a good week for everyone to do solos. The audience went wild. The judges gave a standing ovation. After Nate and the host went over the phone numbers to vote for him, the show went to break. As he left the stage he looked into the audience and I swear he caught my eye and smiled. The rational side of my mind said he must've been looking at someone behind me, but I smiled anyway. I couldn't help myself. His smile was radiant and I liked the idea that it was meant for me.

The last dance of the show belonged to Nate, too. I watched from the wings since my job out front was done. Nate and Barbara danced a Viennese waltz to Celine Dion's "A New Day Has Come." Thirty seconds in I was well past goosebumps as tears ran down my cheeks. It was the most beautiful dance I'd ever seen on the program.

The audience and the judges jumped to their feet and applauded when the music stopped. I joined in, still crying from emotions the dance tapped into. As the duo came downstage to meet up with the host and get their comments, Nate and I locked eyes. I smiled as I continued to clap. His eyes were so alive, sparkling and full of emotion. I felt like I'd just seen a bit of Nate's soul.

Barbara and Nate got their judges' comments, which were extraordinary, and the show signed off for the night. Later, as I was shutting down the power and firing up the on-stage ghost lights, Nate came onto the stage.

"Hey, that dance was... amazing. You deserved everything the judges said."

"Thanks," he said as he bounced with excitement. He was clearly still energized—his eyes were wide, his smile huge. "It came together perfectly. The rehearsals were good, but something about today... it all clicked. I was sort of vibrating inside while we were doing it. It's hard to explain. I thought I might shatter, it was such an all-consuming feeling."

"I think that added to the performance. It was obvious that you and Barbara were moved by what you were doing."

"I'm glad you felt it too. I saw you over there," he said, pointing to the place I'd stood. "I didn't expect to see tears."

I didn't know how to respond. I was a little embarrassed he'd seen that. I'd hoped, since I'd been mostly in the shadows, that he wouldn't have noticed.

I shrugged. "It struck a chord with me. I've never been affected like that before. Touched, yes, but...that was beyond anything I've seen. It made me wish that I could dance, so I could experience what that was like."

"I think everybody's got a little bit of dancer in them, sometimes it just takes a little effort to find it."

"Look at me, I lumber more than anything else."

"You know as well as I do that's just an excuse. You've seen the huge football players dance, right?"

I nodded.

"I bet I can get you waltzing. Let me prove it to you. When are you off again?"

"Thursday."

He dug into his bag and jotted down an address on a slip of paper. "Meet me here at ten Thursday morning. I've got this studio for three hours and we can work on it."

"Don't you have show dances to work on instead of this impossible project?" I asked, gesturing to myself.

"I'll be fine. The studio time is just extra that I have in case I need it. This week some of that can be working with you. Who knows, I might get voted off tomorrow."

"Highly unlikely based on tonight's performances."

"Come on, I want to prove to you that I'm right. Will you let me?"

I loved the idea of hanging out with this guy. It didn't take much for me to agree. "I hope you know what you're in for."

"I think I do." He walked past me, headed for the exit. He turned back before he walked outside and gave me a wave.

FIVE

I WANTED TO BACK OUT. There was no way this could go well. Unfortunately all I had was the address and the time to meet Nate. No phone number to cancel with, and last night I even confirmed with him.

So at ten I climbed three flights of stairs and walked into the reception area of the Michaels & Co. Dance Studio. I told the receptionist I was headed for studio 3B. She pointed the way, not seeming surprised that I was there.

The studio door was closed and a thumping bass line came from inside. I knocked, but no answer. I opened the door a crack and saw Nate going through some hip-hop moves. I stepped in, closed the door and watched. He was focused and didn't stop his work. It was a completely different side of Nate. He was fierce, stomping and locking with aggressive facial expressions. When the music finished he stood still for a moment before turning and giving me his radiant smile, wiping away all the intensity he'd had seconds before.

"You made it."

"You didn't give me much of a choice since you didn't give me a phone number."

"Exactly," he said as he jogged over to me. "This is going to be fun, I promise. No pressure, no judgments. We'll just see how it turns out. Okay?"

"I'm in your hands."

We were quite a picture in the mirror, standing side by side. I had four or five inches on Nate and I was easily twice as wide as him, too. I wasn't fat. Husky was a good description for me. Nate's lean body was on display since he wore a tight sleeveless shirt and shorts that accentuated his sexy ass. I'd dressed for comfort in an old t-shirt and sweat pants.

He went over to his iPod setup, dialed up a slow song I didn't recognize and then returned to stand next to me. "Now we're going to sway a bit. It's gonna help you feel the beat of the music. Watch me, and fall into my rhythm."

He swayed gently back and forth and I was reminded of the rise and fall of the waltz he'd done. I watched for a moment and tried to follow suit. I went left, right, left, watching him closely. I'd get the rhythm for a moment, and just as quickly lose it.

"Try not to over-think it," he said encouragingly.

He didn't break his rhythm while he talked. I struggled. As soon as I had it, I was so happy that I'd mess it up again.

"Don't stop," he said. "I'm going to move behind you and guide your movement."

He put his hands on my hips. His touch was light and his fingers tapped out the beat on each side of me. He pressed up against me and it was suddenly like we were slow dancing.

"One, two, three. Just keep counting in threes."

He set the rhythm and kept counting. Anytime I'd start to get out of rhythm, he'd add pressure against my hips to keep me in time. It was difficult to concentrate with his tight body pushing against mine.

We did variations on this for a good half-hour. He'd be behind me, next to me, sometimes he'd step aside completely and see if I could keep it together without him. Surprisingly, I got better.

"That's looking good."

I came back to a full standing position after having my legs mostly bent during the exercise.

"Yeouch! Now that I've stopped that kinda burns."

"Sorry, I should've warmed you up more. You okay?"

"Yeah, just let me walk it off a bit."

I paced the large studio space, stretching my legs as I went. I was sweating. I didn't expect to sweat from a sway but it was demanding work.

"That's better," I said, after a moment. "What's next?"

"We're going to start moving across the floor. You wearing shorts under those sweats?"

"Yeah. Why?"

"It'll be less restriction on your movement."

I stripped off my sweats and tossed them into a corner. I had on loose basketball shorts that came down to my knee.

"Perfect," he said. "Now we're going to hold each other and move together. Nothing too difficult, moving across the floor with a simple left box step. Watch."

He positioned his hands as if he were holding someone and his feet did the steps with a rise and fall to the motion. When he got to the other end of the room he made the turn by spinning in a couple of circles. He made a complete lap around the studio.

"We're going to do this without music initially. I'll count some of the time. The rest of it, you'll have to keep your own count and follow me. Ready?"

"I hope so."

He smiled a reassuring smile. Standing in front of me, he took my hand in his and put it up high. His other hand went on my waist and I followed suit with my hand on his.

"I'll count to three and then we'll start moving on the next one. Ready?"

I nodded and locked my eyes on his because they were so calm.

We stumbled a couple times as we started. I got better as we went and eventually we sped up as he corrected me less and less.

Holding him felt really good. We weren't super close because there had to be room for the footwork, but there was still a great connection between us. His expressive eyes continued to have a hold on me. I saw a mix of concentration, playfulness, and sexiness. It would be easy to melt in that gaze.

"Do you feel how good you're doing?"

"I think so. Especially the last couple minutes, we moved at a decent pace."

"Yeah, we were and you didn't lose count. I didn't have to say a word." Nate brought us to a stop. "Break time."

We collapsed against the wall opposite the mirrors. I was a sweaty mess. Nate glistened and looked great. He toweled off and tossed me a bottle of water and towel from his bag. How did he know I wouldn't think to bring anything? He was good. Meanwhile, no amount of toweling was going to curtail my sweat. This was more intense than my usual workout. I was going to hurt tomorrow.

I didn't care.

"I'd like to teach you the basic waltz from the other night. I want to prove to you that you're getting the rhythm for it. Some of it I'll leave out because the moves would require weeks more of training, no offense."

"None taken. You've gotten me further than I thought possible already."

"So let's get you even further. Anytime you need to stop, you tell me."

I hopped up from my cross-legged sitting position. "Let's do it."

I put my hand out to help him up. I pulled him up

and he leapt off the floor and landed right in front of me. His eyes transfixed me again. I stared, unable to look away. I could hardly breathe, his gaze was so intense.

The moment must have thrown him, too. I heard it in his voice as his confidence faltered for a moment. "Um, okay...well here's what we're going to do. I've got the music and it'll be running on a loop. We won't stop. I'll talk us through what we're doing and I'll lead like I have been."

I took a deep breath. I felt safe in his hands. I had no doubt that he was going to make this work and that it would be pretty freakin' cool.

He went to the iPod and started the music. Nate put his hands up as we'd practiced—as I'd seen him do two days before with Barbara—and I placed mine to match. He counted softly. We did two counts of three holding each other, swaying like we'd done earlier.

"After the next three count we're going to start moving to your left. Try to stay bouncy on your toes. It'll make you lighter on your feet. Here it comes. One, two, three."

And we were off. It took me a few counts to get into the music. He kept counting and we moved. As we headed to the corner, he squeezed on my right hand and I knew we were going to turn to the right. I remembered the turns in the dance and how they spun around anytime they needed to change direction.

The next time Nate declared a break, I looked at the clock and was shocked that another half-hour had gone by. It seemed like only a couple of minutes. We went straight for the water bottles.

"You're doing really good," he said between drinks.

He smiled and I got quivery inside. It may not have been a perfect waltz, but he got me to move in a way that resembled a dance. It was like I was floating.

"I've got a good teacher," I said, finishing the bottle of water and running the towel over my head. "It's incredible that you've pulled this off."

He gave a shy grin and shrugged. It was the same look he had when the judges praised him. "This was nothing. You ready for it to get more complicated?"

"Really? You want to keep going?"

He nodded and I had an idea what was coming next. I was game for it. At this point, he could convince me to do anything.

"Let's give it a go."

He took his place in front of me and we got into the hold we'd been using. "We're going to do what we've already practiced once and then go past it. We're going to see how much more you can do. Do your best to just let me lead you and I'll talk you through it."

We did the parts I'd already learned and it was good.

"Here comes the new part," he said.

He subtly pushed and pulled me and I did my best to keep up and do what the dance required. I'd re-watched the waltz a lot since Nate performed it, and even though I could see it in my head, my body wasn't cooperating. It finally got too complicated and I stumbled.

Damn it.

My feet weren't paying attention. Nate wasn't panicking. He tried to guide me back to what I should be doing. He slowed us down, too.

"Come on Todd, you can do this," he said, sounding nothing but encouraging. "It's just the box step with some extra flourishes."

The focus in his eyes overwhelmed me. Rather than drive me to get my feet corrected, it distracted me. My left foot tripped over my right, the momentum carried me forward, and there was nothing I could do but fall. I toppled on top of Nate. I was large enough that I nearly covered him entirely.

"Shit. Sorry. Are you okay?"

Before I could roll off him, Nate put his arms around me.

"What are you doing?"

"This is nice. You on top of me."

I laughed. "Seriously? I must be squashing you."

"I'm small, but I'm not that delicate."

I felt him getting aroused against my stomach. He didn't seem the slightest bit embarrassed; instead, there was a fire in his eyes. It fueled a stirring in my shorts. Embarrassment washed over me. This wasn't some hookup. This was supposed to be a dance lesson. I gently moved, trying to break his hold on me.

Nate tightened his grip. He wasn't letting me up, at least not without a struggle.

"Shouldn't we get up?"

"I already told you, I like you right here." His voice was low and sexy.

"Okay, have it your way." I smiled, ignored the embarrassment, and placed a soft kiss on his lips. The energy from the kiss surged through me, almost as if it was my first kiss ever.

"I've wanted you to do that since the first day I saw you on set," Nate said.

I grinned. "I've fantasized about you since the first time I saw you dance across my TV screen. I never thought we'd end up in the same room, much less like this."

This time he brought his head up so he could kiss me. He pushed his tongue into my mouth and we kissed deeply. I maneuvered so we were side-by-side, holding each other. At least this way I didn't feel like I was too much of a weight on him. The kissing continued until the alarm on his phone went off.

"Fuck," Nate said, softly. I'd never heard him swear before, not even during the most insane dress rehearsal. Thankfully the alarm only lasted a few seconds.

"What?"

"Barbara and I have to meet a choreographer. I have to go," he said, but he still didn't move. "Have a late dinner with me?"

He planted a bunch of small kisses on my lips, cheeks, chin. A contented sigh escaped my lips. He knew exactly how to get what he wanted. "I'll meet you wherever, whenever."

"I know just the place if I can get a reservation. I'll text you the info."

He gave me one more quick kiss. I stood and then helped him up. We kissed again and stepped into each other. He closed his eyes as a low hum emanated from him.

The phone alarm rang out again.

He cursed, under his breath this time, and shook his head in frustration as he went over to his bag and dug out the phone to silence it. "Why couldn't you have fallen earlier?" He winked at me.

I went to where he was packing things into his bag and grabbed his phone off the floor. I entered myself into his contacts list.

"Have a good rehearsal," I said, handing the phone back. "You've got my number, so let me know where and when to meet you."

"I will," he said before kissing me. "Rehearsal will not go fast enough."

He bolted out of the studio.

SIX

As REQUESTED, I arrived at the Harmony Club at nine-thirty sharp. The place billed itself as a ballroom dinner club. I was intrigued and was checking the menu outside when Nate arrived. He looked stunning in a pair of fitted jeans, a whiter-than-white t-shirt and a black vest.

"It's so good to see you." Nate gave me a quick kiss. He smelled great, a combination of soap and just a hint of cologne. I wanted to bury my head in his chest to take it all in.

"You're in a good mood," I said, watching him as he vibrated with energy. "How was rehearsal?"

"Outstanding. This new choreographer is trying to kill us, but if we can pull this off it'll be great. What'd you do with the rest of your day?"

A warm, tingly feeling washed over me. I've never had a guy this interested in me. It was overwhelming, exciting and completely fantastic.

"I ran some errands and then got lazy in front of the TV. Plus, had to relax my legs a bit. That was a helluva workout you gave me."

Nate took my hand as we went into the club. A large dance floor sat in the middle of the room, with tables and booths on all sides. The colors were very stylish, mostly black, white and gray with random punches of reds and blues. Some people were dining while others were out on the floor. I couldn't take my eyes off all the different couples dancing.

"Cool, right?" Nate asked, seeing the look on my face.

"Very. I didn't know this place was even here."

An older gentleman in a finely tailored black suit greeted Nate at the maître d' stand. "Ahhh, Nathaniel, I saw your name in the book. It's good to see you. Your usual table?"

"Actually, if you've got something closer to the dance floor that would be great."

"Very good. Follow me, please."

We moved off to our table, which turned out to be right on the rail next to the dance floor.

"Who is joining you tonight?" he asked as he gave us menus.

"Mr. Katz, this is Todd Stewart. He works on the show and I've been teaching him to waltz."

"Good to meet you, Todd. Maybe we'll see you on the floor tonight?"

"I don't know about that," I said, feeling self-conscious.

"We'll see," Nate said, giving me a wink.

"I take it you come here a lot?" I asked after the maître d' left.

"Not as often as I'd like. Mr. Katz and my father went to Berkeley together so when I came out here my dad recommended I check this place out. He knew I'd love it. But you know the schedule I keep."

"I'm glad you brought me," I said, taking his hand. "I can't believe I'm here. The past couple days have been unbelievable. Actually meeting you and watching you dance live was amazing enough, but now you're teaching me to dance. We're at dinner. Hell, we've made out and might have done more if it weren't for that obnoxious phone of yours."

He laughed.

"You're shaking," he said, squeezing my hand tighter.

"It's a lot for me to process. And I'm a little nervous. I can't believe a nobody techie like me is sitting across from someone as attractive and talented as you."

"You know, your union probably wouldn't want you to call yourself a nobody techie—and neither do I." His eyes were gorgeous, sparkling from the table's candlelight as he spoke. "Seriously, though, you are completely my kind of man. Like I told you this morning, from the first time I saw you, I knew I had to know you. I bet I'm just as nervous as you are."

We sat there staring into each other's eyes. His thumb caressed the hairs on the back of my hand.

"Hi, I'm Joseph and I'll be serving you tonight." That brought us back to reality and we quickly made our selections. Nate went with a chicken Caesar salad and I went straight for a steak. We each got a single glass of wine, knowing that Nate had to be ready for a full day of rehearsals tomorrow.

"Have a go at the dance floor before we eat?" he suddenly asked.

"Out there? With all those people?" I gave him a look like he was crazy.

"Yes, with all those people. It'll be fine. I won't let anything bad happen." He extended his hand across the table. "It won't be anything difficult. Just follow my lead and it'll be good. No, it'll be great."

I could do this. There's no way he'd try the complicated moves that brought us tumbling down earlier. Nate led me out to the floor.

"You ready?"

I nodded. Vanessa Carlton's "Ordinary Day" played and I struggled to latch on to the right rhythm.

"Relax," he said, shaking my shoulders gently. "This is going to be fun."

He put his hands on me in the same position they'd been that morning. Once Nate took hold of me, my nervousness evaporated. I was engulfed by his dance-floor confidence, which protected me like a shield. He counted to four, softly, so only I could hear him. He stepped to me with his right foot and I stepped back with my left and we were moving.

I grinned stupidly. This was going well. We got

through "Ordinary Day" doing basic foxtrot moves. Nate moved us effortlessly around the floor, navigating us between the other couples.

"If It Kills Me" by Jason Mraz played next. Nate had done a complicated contemporary jazz piece to this song the second week of the show. I struggled with the shift in rhythm. Nate must have felt the lapse in my footwork as he softly counted again.

I loved that he did that.

"Do you trust me?" Nate asked.

I nodded apprehensively. I didn't want to mess this up.

"Let me know if this is too much." This song had very different musicality from the first, and Nate took advantage of that to move us from the smoothness of the foxtrot into something with sharper moves. It was thrilling to be led this way. I couldn't tell what style we were doing. I lost myself in the moves, the music and Nate.

The Mraz song ended and Nate danced us over to the edge of the floor.

"Our food just arrived," he said. "We can get back out there later."

We held hands going back to the table. I couldn't believe how well that had gone. It was the most thrilling thing I'd ever done.

"My God that was cool," I said, barely able to contain my excitement. "Thank you."

"You were great."

"Really? You'd tell me the truth, right?"

"You followed very well, not pushing back on me. You went where I wanted us to go. You got off the beat sometimes, but you recovered. I only had to count twice, which is good. Most importantly, I loved having you in my arms."

"Does dancing always feel like that?" I asked after I swallowed a bite of steak.

"Like what?"

"Exhilarating. Intoxicating."

"Yeah. Exactly." He crunched on salad as he talked. "That's how I felt doing the waltz this week. It also happens when I dance with someone special."

"No wonder I feel like I'm going to explode, the dance and the partner were perfect."

We ate for a few minutes in comfortable silence.

"So what happens for you when the show's over?" I asked.

Nate took a sip of wine while he contemplated his answer. "Well, hopefully I stay on for the next four weeks. I want to win. But even if I don't, I'm determined to make it to the last show. Since I made top ten, I'm committed to the tour this fall. After that I've got offers to consider. There's a Broadway revival of a Fosse show next spring that I've been invited to audition for. It'd be incredible to be part of that. I'm also seriously considering the judges' suggestion that I return to a company so I can continue to grow. One in San Francisco has already contacted me. I'd love to choreograph too, maybe even come back and do it on the show. It's kinda daunting when I think the next step could define what my career is."

He took another bite as his expression shifted from serious to more mischievous. I was intrigued, and continued eating so he would finish the thought he was obviously forming.

"Plus there's this guy," Nate said, leaning in closer to whisper. "I need to figure out what's going on there."

"Funny you should say that. I just started seeing somebody too, and I'm falling for him pretty fast."

After the mutual revelation, we moved to safer topics. I told him how I got started in electrical as an apprentice to my dad. I casually mentioned that I could probably go back and pick up a job in New York since my dad still worked on Broadway. He told me how his parents enrolled him in dance class at age four because he wouldn't stop moving. They wanted him to channel that energy somewhere and he kept going right through college with it.

We finished dinner, but delayed dessert because I wanted to dance again. I couldn't believe I asked Nate this time. A ballad played and he pulled me close when we got on the floor. This left me confused about what to do with my hands. His went across the middle of my back.

"Just put your arms around me," he said, resting his head on my shoulder.

Standing so close, we couldn't move across the floor, so Nate kept us swaying in place and occasionally turning small circles.

"You feel so good," he said, as he pressed closer.

I savored the moment so I'd be able to remember every detail. I didn't care about anything else. As the song changed to something more upbeat, Nate lifted his head, looked me in the eyes and, without a single word, kissed me.

We danced for well over an hour. As the songs played, Nate changed how we moved and I kept up reasonably well. We kissed a lot, too. My body was electrified from the excitement and growing lust as our kisses got longer and more passionate. I expected Mr. Katz to come onto the dance floor and tell us to get a room.

When it seemed like we were doing more kissing than actual dancing, I decided we'd had enough foreplay.

"We should get out of here," I said, but didn't release my hold on him.

"Yeah," he said between kisses. "I live close by, but I also have Kyle and Devin as roommates."

"I'm about five minutes from here. I can drive and bring you back to your car later, that way you don't have to follow."

"Let's go."

We stopped at the table long enough for us both to throw down cash, hoping we'd covered the bill that we weren't waiting for. I steered us to the door.

"Mr. Katz, thank you for a great night," Nate said as we passed the maître d'. "If we didn't leave enough, let me know next time."

My truck was parked four blocks away and we practically sprinted there hand-in-hand. As I unlocked his door, Nate pushed me against the truck, laid his whole body against mine and kissed me hard. I moaned into his mouth. The kiss was explosive.

"Need you bad," he said.

"Get in and let's go," I said as I pushed him back so I could get us on the road.

Luckily no police were around as I dodged my way through North Hollywood traffic to get to my small house in record time.

"Nice place," Nate said as we cut across my small, tidy front yard. As we got to the door, I fumbled and dropped the keys because I was moving too fast. As soon as we were in and the door was closed he pushed me against the foyer wall, just like he'd done against the truck.

His mouth was on mine. I happily ate up his aggressive kisses. We needed to get to the bedroom. It was time to use my size to my advantage. I reached around Nate, grabbed just under his butt and picked him up, holding him close. He wrapped his legs and arms around me.

"Oooh. I like this," he said, adjusting himself so he could kiss me as we traveled through the house. "I'm going to have to teach you how to do lifts so you can pick me up and twirl me around the dance floor."

"Hit the light switch," I said as we entered the bedroom. "I want to see you out of those clothes."

He did as he was told and I lowered him to the bed.

I opened his jeans as he unbuttoned and tossed away his vest before raising himself up so I could pull his jeans and briefs off. It all worked perfectly until I ran into his shoes. Luckily, they were easy to slip off. As I finally got his lower half stripped, Nate sat up and pulled off his t-shirt.

I stood at the foot of the bed and studied him. He was propped up on his elbows and his abs were sharply defined. His smooth chest and arms were flexed, giving me a good look at his muscles. Those powerful legs that had been wrapped around me were incredible, all the muscles perfectly sculpted. He'd exposed a lot of skin on the show, dancing in shorts and shirtless from time to time, but to see the entire package laid out for me was breathtaking.

"You're gorgeous."

"I'm glad you think so," he said, giving me his shy smile. He pushed himself up so he sat in front of me. "Gotta get you naked too."

I practically ripped the buttons on my shirt as I hastily got rid of it. In no time, I was naked. He pulled me down on top of him, and it reminded me of how I'd fallen on him earlier. At least it wasn't an uncontrolled fall this time.

Nate and I traded positions several times as we got to know each other intimately. Our bodies had no trouble with the choreography as we figured out where each other's pleasure points were. By the time we were done, we were sweaty and spent.

"Incredible," Nate said after a kiss. "I've never been worked over like that. I don't think I can move."

I lay at his side, my arm over his chest and his leg over mine. "You could stay here tonight and we wouldn't have to move at all."

"We'd have to get up early, I've got rehearsal at seven."

"We can make that work." I got up to kill the light, set the clock for six and then settled back in bed, wrapping myself around Nate.

"It feels so good in your arms. I already know I'm not going to want to get up," he said as he turned to give me a kiss on the nose. "Sleep good, my sexy big man."

SEVEN

MORE THAN A WEEK after dance class and our date, Nate and I were seeing each other as much as we could. We'd had a couple more waltz lessons and he swore I was getting better. I took his word for it. He videoed part of our session and I admit that it didn't look as bad as I thought it would. Sometimes I still felt like an elephant trying to look graceful next to a swan. He stayed over at my place a couple of nights, too.

I worked Saturday morning on a multi-panel light-up backdrop. The specs were complex and I was holed up in the rear of the soundstage where I could spread out across several work benches.

"Todd!" It was Martin. "You here?"

"Yeah, in the back." I kept working as I waited for him, wiring the frame I'd received from the scenic department.

"There you are. Been looking for you all morning."

I'd been here since a little before call time and not

only did he have my cell number, he could reach me on walkie-talkie from anywhere on the lot.

"What's up?"

"Have you seen this?" He angrily shoved his tablet into my hands.

There were pictures of Nate and me at the Harmony Club. It looked like someone took pictures on their phone and sent them off to one of the gossip sites. You couldn't see my face as they were more focused on Nate's. If you knew me though, you probably recognized me. "*ANTD's* Nathaniel Steps Out... With a Man" read the headline.

Fuck.

"No. Didn't know about that."

"So it is you."

"Yup," I said. I wasn't going to deny it. If I did, it'd eventually come out anyway. My phone buzzed in my pocket, interrupting me. I pulled it out as I continued. "Is that a problem? As far as I know there's nothing that says I can't go to dinner with a contestant."

It was a text from Nate. I swiped to see what he said. *Did you see this? We're famous.* He had a link that I didn't click since I had a good idea that I'd just seen it.

"Well, no. But come on, Todd. He's what? Eighteen? Nineteen? How's that going to look? Not just for him, but you and the show."

"For starters, he's coming up on twenty-five. But even if he were eighteen, he'd still be an adult and it's my business, not yours. Second, he seems pretty okay with it since I just got a text from him asking if I'd seen it. As for the show, I don't think the rules state who the dancers can and can't date. And I know it's not in my contract."

Martin was furious. I'd never seen him like this, and I didn't like it.

"Have you considered what it could do for his chances of winning? What're the voters going to think?"

I hadn't thought of that. I didn't know if Nate had, either. I certainly didn't want to hurt his career, but I also didn't want to give him up. We were still getting to know each other.

"What's really going on here, Martin?" I stopped working and looked at him. "It's not like you're just finding out I'm gay, 'cause you've known that a long time."

His nose flared. He reminded me of an angry cartoon character. I wouldn't have been surprised if smoke billowed from his ears.

"I brought you to this show. I expected you to come in, do the job as long as they needed you, and then go back to your hiatus. Instead, you're putting the show in the paper in unflattering ways and potentially affecting the outcome of the season."

"Is this from you, or someone on the show? While I'm working here, technically I'm under Jordan and Clive's supervision. They should be telling me if there's a problem. People here have known for a few days we're seeing each other."

"Break it off before someone gets hurt, okay?"

His tone was deflated. Something I said took the bluster out of him. Without another word he left the same way he came.

I went back to my phone and clicked the link Nate sent. It was the same set of pics that Martin showed me. I laughed. I'd never been snapped by paparazzi before. It was kinda cool.

I rang up Nate, hoping I'd catch him on a break.

"Hey, sexy," he said. I could tell he was smiling.

"Hey. So we're famous. Is that okay by you?"

"Sure. Unexpected getting caught there, but whatever. I suppose we should be happy they didn't get us making out at your truck."

I lowered my voice. This didn't need to get spread all over the sound stage again like it had during Martin's rant. "I got an earful from Martin just now about how this was potentially bad for you and the show. Like it might not go over well with the voters."

"Fuck that. And who's Martin anyway?"

"He's a friend, or at least I thought he was. He got me the job here."

"I'll be honest, before we went to dinner, I read over my contract and the rules. There's nothing that says we can't date. And if it means people don't vote for me, well screw them." We were quiet for a moment. "Are you okay with this?"

"Yeah," I said.

"Okay. I was worried about the silence."

"Sorry, just thinking. I don't want to damage your

chances on the show, or your career. But I don't want to stop seeing you either."

"Then it's settled. We keep doing what we're doing."

He wasn't worried about the show or his career, so I guess I shouldn't be either.

"Nate, you coming?" I heard Barbara call out in the distance.

"Yup. I gotta go practice some moves. I'll see you later."

"Yes you will. Later, Nate."

He clicked off. That went better than I thought it would. He'd thought about this a lot if he'd checked his contract. I should probably check mine just to make sure everything was as okay as I thought it was.

EIGHT

I LOVED WORKING ON *ANTD*. The longer I did, the sadder I got, knowing it was going to end, likely before the season was over. It was challenging work as everyone in the creative departments constantly pushed the envelope.

Even when I was working with my dad on New York shows, it was a matter of setting something up and then simply maintaining it. Here there was no maintenance. Something existed for a matter of days before it was gone. There were only a few props left intact if it was thought they might get used for the finale. Other than that, a part of Friday mornings was spent breaking things down.

Surprisingly for a Saturday, I finished on time. It was only seven-thirty as I turned on to my street. It was a treat to see Nate's small, blue Honda parked in front of my house. I hadn't expected to see him this early. Saturdays were usually packed with rehearsals, first with the choreographers and then working with their partners. Last week he'd come over around eleven and we cuddled for a while before he crashed.

As I pulled into the driveway, he jumped up from the porch steps and came over to my truck. He had an easy smile on his face and looked fairly energetic, which was surprising given the physical day he must've had.

"Hey," I said, getting out. He stepped into me and we hugged. "I didn't know you were going to be here. Hope you haven't waited long."

"Maybe fifteen minutes. I called the studio and they told me you'd left already, so I came here. Barbara's grabbing dinner with her parents so we're doing our practice later. I decided to come surprise you instead."

Wow. He could've done any number of things, not to mention resting, and he decided to come here. I'm not sure what I did to deserve him.

"Do you want to go get some dinner? I just need to clean up."

"Already covered. It'll be here in a few minutes. I ordered up some Chinese. Hope that's okay."

"Absolutely." I grabbed his hand and we walked to the front door. "Kinda perfect actually. I was thinking about Chinese already. You must've read my mind."

"Excellent," he said as I unlocked the door and let us in. "Why don't you get cleaned up? It should be here when you're done."

"Why don't you shower with me?" I winked at him and he actually blushed for a moment.

"Normally I'd jump on that, but one of us needs to be dry and clothed when the food gets here."

I couldn't fault his logic. Maybe there'd be time to get him naked after dinner.

"I s'pose you're right. I'll be quick." I headed back to the bedroom and he followed. "What're you doing?"

"Just because I'm not getting in the shower doesn't mean I can't watch."

"Oh, I see. That's how this works?"

I stripped off my t-shirt and threw it at him. He surprised me by covering his face with it and inhaling.

"Damn, maybe I shouldn't have ordered food," he said once he tossed the shirt into the hamper.

I shook my head and smiled at him. "You're bad." I sat on the bed and quickly got out of my work boots and socks. "How was rehearsal?"

He leaned against the doorframe as I finished stripping. "I'm not sure Barbara and I are built for the salsa. So many turns and flips. It's the craziest thing I've done. We're hoping we get it figured out tonight so we're not falling on each other tomorrow."

"Somehow I can't picture you falling, either one of you falling, for that matter." I headed to the shower and he followed, grabbing at my ass as we went.

"I'm sure everyone will see it on Tuesday. There's no way they're not going to use some of that in the rehearsal package. We both had some pretty righteous falls as we got tangled up."

"At least she can't squash you," I said, stepping into a warm spray of water.

"Hmmmm. You realize that's one of my favorite memories, right? I loved you on top of me. Why do you think I position myself so some of your weight's on me if we're lying down? It just feels right."

"If you say so." I poked my head around the shower curtain to find him sitting on the vanity. "As long as I don't completely flatten you, I guess it's okay."

"Like I said, I'm not as delicate as I look."

"Yeah, but you're not steel reinforced either."

He stuck his tongue out at me and I retreated behind the curtain. The sooner I was done, the sooner I could properly enjoy his company. The doorbell rang and I heard his shoes hit the floor as he jumped off the counter.

"I'm gonna get that. I'll serve the food, you hurry up. Okay?"

"You got it. I'll be out in a minute."

It was nice. Finding him waiting. I could get used to this. I finished up just as the front door closed. I heard him in the kitchen getting plates out of the cupboard while I toweled off.

As I arrived in the kitchen, dressed in sweats and a t-shirt, he'd already laid out plates piled with fried rice, some kind of beef and vegetable dish, and chow mein. Our tastes in Chinese food were similar. He had poured himself a glass of water.

"Do you want water, Coke, or something else?"

"I'll get it," I said going to the fridge to get the Coke. "Go ahead and sit."

He plopped down and I had to stare for a moment.

"What?" he asked.

"I was trying to think when I ate at the table last. I usually crash on the couch in front of the TV."

"We can, if you'd rather." He picked up his plate.

"No, this is actually a great change of pace." I sat down and emptied my can of soda into the glass Nate had left next to my plate. "I'm glad you thought of this."

"I was hoping it'd be okay if I just showed up."

"Anytime. I can't imagine that I wouldn't be thrilled to see you."

He smiled and it gave me goosebumps.

"So can I ask you," he said, fixing his eyes on mine, which of course got my attention, "why has no one snapped you up?"

I shrugged. It was a question my friends asked a lot. "Haven't really been looking. Just got into a routine of work and hanging out with friends. I'm not big on going out on my own. Sometimes my friend Paul will try to hook me up with a date, but I just haven't found *the guy*. What about you? Young, talented, hot as hell."

He looked at his plate for a moment in one of those rare moments his confidence seemingly faltered. "I dated and messed around a lot in college, especially early on. But by the time I was a senior, I was kinda burned out on it. Once I graduated, I went into a dance company, and that's where my focus was. I know it's going to continue to be a focus, but I'd like something more, too. I hope I can figure out how to strike that balance so I've got someone to come home to."

"It was so much easier in school, wasn't it?" I asked between bites. "Be in love for a couple weeks, screw around…"

"Right?" He said emphatically. "I think I've become more selective, too. A guy might be smokin' hot, but if he can't hold a conversation or is too self-absorbed, it doesn't matter how good the sex might be. I can get myself off just fine, thank you. Where was school for you?"

"I did some community college for a few semesters, but I didn't graduate. It wasn't for me. I knew I wanted to do what my dad did, so I got into a trade program and then apprenticed."

"I'd love to meet your dad sometime, since he's kinda responsible for me meeting you."

I loved that he didn't seem bothered that I hadn't graduated from college. I'd been with a couple of guys who couldn't get past that.

"If nothing else, I can make sure you guys meet when you're in New York on the tour. Hell, he might even be part of the local crew that helps with it."

"That would be pretty awesome if that was the case." Nate filled his plate again, having demolished his first helping.

"What about you?"

"Florida State. I double-majored in dance and

education. I wanted to have a backup in case dancing didn't work out. So far so good though," he grinned.

"That might be an understatement."

He was so level-headed. I hadn't expected to hear anything but pursuing dance, but he had backup plans. It meshed with what he'd said on our first date about weighing his post-show options.

"I love this house," he said out of nowhere. "It's not too big, not too small. Your decorating is minimal but comfortable and tidy."

"Thanks. Once I figured out I was going to be based here, I saved up and bought it. I like not sharing walls with neighbors. Plus it's a little something that's mine, you know?"

"Yeah. The quiet's nice. There's always something going on where the show has us. We're not the only show staying in those apartments. Some dating show has people there, too. I don't know how the regular residents of that building deal with it. At least *ANTD* doesn't shoot us there, but I've seen the other show's cameras there at all hours."

"That would get old fast."

We'd plowed through the food. The conversation was wonderful, getting to know each other better.

"Come with me," I said, grabbing his hand. We went into the living room and I slid the curtains back to reveal a sliding glass door that went out to the back yard.

"It just gets better," he said. "This is nice."

The patio had a small grill and while the grass had

seen better days, thanks to the drought, everything was still well-kept. Most of the yard was in shade, with the sun on the other side of the house. The fence was high enough that only the house to the right could see the yard from their second floor. I led him to the hammock.

"Welcome to one of my favorite getaways." I lay back in it. "Join me?"

"Hell yeah." He kicked off his sneakers and pulled his socks off, setting them inside his shoes.

He snuggled in next to me and we stayed there, talking, as the sun set. He only left when Barbara texted him that she was headed to the studio. As he left, I gave him a key so he could come back after he finished with Barbara, and any other time he wanted to.

NINE

SUNDAY BROUGHT DRESS REHEARSALS, camera blocking and activity all over the soundstage. Dancers who were not on stage were usually practicing in some out-of-the-way corner. The tech crew was doing what was needed to be ready for tomorrow night.

I was working above the stage with a guy from the lighting crew to make sure each dance was lit to the specifications of the choreographer and director. Roman selected the lights we needed and got them focused on the stage, and I got them wired into the grid correctly.

I was surprised at how much I could focus on my work. The dancers, including Nate, were right below us and I managed to keep my attention on the work. I'd already seen some of Nate's partner performance for the week, and he gave me a private performance of his solo last night before we went to sleep.

Nothing more had come of Martin's blow up. Nate

and I were in a routine where we would leave the studio together each evening, or I'd pick him up from wherever he was rehearsing. We'd grab dinner and maybe go dancing for a while. Some nights we'd just hang out at my place so he could relax.

On stage, the dancers worked through the opening number. At week eight, there were six in the competition. We were done with lighting as they went through it, so I could allow myself a moment to watch. I had no trouble picking Nate out from the group, and not just because I knew *exactly* what he looked like, but I could pick out his dance style, too. He was performing what the choreographer designed, but it had his unique flair.

"You've fallen hard, haven't you?" Roman asked.

I didn't know Roman well, so his question was a little embarrassing. "Didn't know it was that obvious."

"It happens at least once a season," he said. "Someone hooks up. It's usually between the dancers, though. I can't remember a dancer getting together with a techie. You give all of us hope."

He smiled at me and elbowed my side. It sounded almost creepy coming from him. I hoped it wasn't coming off that way to the others. Martin had certainly tried to make an issue out of the age difference between us.

"It was a surprise to me, too," I said, trying to change the tone of the conversation. "It just happened. We started talking, then talked some more and we ended up going out. Hopefully it's more than a show fling."

"Wow. I wouldn't know what to talk to them about. How'd you..."

"Yeow!"

I looked down to see what happened. Nate was lying on the stage, holding his leg just above his ankle. The playback hadn't stopped and dancers in the front were still going, while the ones nearest Nate came to his aid.

"Stop the playback!" I shouted into my walkie-talkie. "We've got an injury, medic to the stage."

The music stopped at the same time the choreographer leapt up on the stage. The main lights came on as well, illuminating everything. I bolted for the ladder down to stage level as the medical staff arrived.

The area around Nate was crowded. The director was on stage now, too, while the dancers were being moved back to give him space. I didn't have any reason to get closer, but I did want him to know I was there.

I stood behind the dancers. His view of me was blocked, but I stayed where I was. Barbara, however, saw me and moved to my side.

"Did you see what happened?" she asked. We hadn't talked much, so it was nice of her to come over.

"No. I was working above. I only heard him cry out."

"It looked like he came down on his foot wrong. These kinds of things happen all the time. I'm sure he'll be fine."

The choreographer and medic had him under the

arms and helped him stand. Nate gently put weight on the foot and flinched.

"Dammit," he said, his voice carrying through the soundstage.

Barbara was right. I'd seen this happen on the dance shows. Dancers were good at recovery and this show had a great medical staff. I also knew Nate was strong.

Nate kept his foot off the floor as he was walked off the stage. He and I locked eyes briefly and all I saw was irritation. By the time he got into the wings, a wheelchair was there for him. The choreographer came back on stage and told everyone they'd find out how Nate was after he'd been examined.

"Robert," the choreographer called into the seating area, "come take Nate's place in the routine so we can get the run-through done."

A young man came down from the bleachers and jumped up on the stage. I recognized him as a former contestant. He must have been assisting this choreographer. The other dancers were getting into position. Barbara squeezed my arm before she went back to her mark.

"Thanks," I said, and then quickly moved off the stage.

In the wings, I couldn't find Nate. I was torn between seeing what was up and going back to work. Professionalism won out. Hanging around medical wouldn't help anything. Not being in my place for tech rehearsal would slow things down for everyone else. I climbed back up and found Roman exactly where I'd left him.

"What'd you hear?"

"Not much. Looks like a foot injury."

I pulled my phone out and texted Nate: *Hope you're okay. I'm up in the lights. If you need something, text me and I'll come.*

We got a request to throw a bunch of white light against the backdrop and that gave us something to do for about fifteen minutes. It was a welcome distraction.

After the group number was done and the lighting and camera blocking locked in, lunch was called.

"See you back here in thirty," Roman said as he went to store some of the extra lights we had out. I grabbed a couple and followed him to the lockers. "You don't have to do that."

"I don't mind. Get you a few extra minutes on lunch."

He was right, I didn't have to do it, but I liked helping where I could. We had the extra equipment put away in just a few minutes.

Once we got to stage level, I saw Nate talking to Barbara near one of the makeup tables.

"Hey," he said as soon as he saw me. He waved me over. From the sound of his voice, I wouldn't have guessed he was hurt. The wrappings on his foot and the crutch he held gave it away.

"Good to see you," I said as I got to him.

"Mind if I use you as a crutch?" he asked. He

nestled himself against my side, using me to hold himself up instead of the actual crutch he had.

"Not at all." I wrapped my arm around him to stabilize him more.

"I was letting Barbara know the plan for the rest of the day." He turned back to her. "So you and I will walk through our number for lighting and blocking. Wally will dance it with you and review the footage to sign off on the lights and stuff. I'll walk my solo for lighting. They think if it stays wrapped and I ice it for the rest of the day that I'll be good for tomorrow."

She nodded. "I hope so. I like Wally, but you and I've got the chemistry so I'll be praying for the healing."

"Me too," he said, releasing me to give her a hug.

"You guys coming to lunch?" she asked.

"Yeah," Nate said. "We'll be right behind you."

She gracefully darted away. Most people moved quickly at lunch time since it was a strict thirty minutes.

"Thanks for the text, and for letting me lean."

"Of course. Shall I escort you to lunch?"

"I'd like that." He grinned at me.

We walked carefully across the stage. I thought about doing something extra-chivalrous like carrying him. But that would make it too much of a big deal when we got to the lunch line.

"Is it okay that I didn't come back with you? I wasn't sure what you'd want."

"You did exactly what you should've. Even before

you texted me, I knew if I said that I needed you that you'd come."

We kept talking as we hobbled to where the catering truck was set up just outside one of the exit doors. "Do you think you'll be ready tomorrow?"

"I expect to be good enough to dance. There's an option to sit out for a week and let the votes carry me through. I'd rather not take that chance, especially this close to the end. I want to give people a reason to vote, so unless the doc and I think there's a risk of doing more damage, I plan to be on stage at five tomorrow."

I liked his resolve. He wasn't going to take an out unless he had to, and then only to protect himself from long-term injury.

"Want me to grab you something?" I said, seeing there was a bit of a line. "You can sit, get the leg up."

"That'd be great," he said. "Right here's fine." We were next to a table where no one was sitting, so I let him settle himself. "Just grab me a salad with some chicken, vinaigrette dressing and some water, please. And if you can, a bag of ice."

"You got it."

I ended up next to Roman in line. "How'd you end up way back here when we got down at the same time?"

"Shhh," he said, with a smirk, "I'm back for seconds." We both laughed. "They've got really good lasagna today."

"Nice," I said. "Now I know what I'm having."

"How's Nate?" he asked. I quickly explained the

situation. "Man, these dancers are tough. I've only seen a couple exit due to injury. They'll fight through anything."

In short order, I had our food stacked up on a tray and was on my way back to the table. Barbara was there, as was Devin, one of Nate's roommates. They'd left a chair for me.

"Devin, this is Todd, my boyfriend," Nate said. It was the first time he'd introduced me as his boyfriend and I liked it a lot.

"Good to meet you officially," Devin said. "I've seen you around, of course."

"Nice to meet you, too," I said as I distributed food. "I've enjoyed watching you dance."

"Watch out," Devin said, "Nate might get jealous if you start complimenting other guys." He smirked at Nate.

"He can compliment whomever he wants. I know he's my biggest fan." Nate positioned the ice bag on his ankle and started prepping his salad.

Barbara just shook her head at us.

"All this male posturing, I may have to switch tables." She turned to me and changed the subject. "I hear he's teaching you our waltz."

"He's *trying to*, is more accurate," I said. "It's nothing like what you two did, not even close."

"He lies," Nate said. "It's coming along. My goal is to have it down for the wrap party so we can dance it together."

This was a surprise to me. "What?"

"Cool," said Barbara.

"Oh, no. No way you're getting me to dance in front of everyone, and especially not your original partner."

"Remember, you have to trust me."

"Trust him," Barbara said. "He'll take care of you. He's a great partner."

My phone buzzed and I looked at the display. It was the production office.

"I need to take this, I'll be right back."

I walked away from the tables to where I wouldn't be heard. I expected the worst. Maybe Martin had finally made a bigger deal out of me and Nate dating. I hadn't spoken to him since he came down on me.

Turned out it wasn't bad, just disappointing. The guy I was subbing for was coming back at the start of the next production week.

Damn.

I returned to the table and Nate saw the disappointment on my face.

"Everything okay?" he asked.

"Yeah, sorry." I perked myself up. It wasn't like this was unexpected. "Just found out that I'm back on hiatus after this week. The guy I'm filling in for will be back on Friday."

"Awww, really?" Nate asked.

"You'll just have to come watch the live shows then," Devin said.

"I love watching you guys and it'll be nice to do it without having to work at the same time."

"Five minutes until we're back," came the voice over the PA. "We'll start with a walk through for Nathaniel and Barbara. Five minutes, please, for on-stage talent and all tech crew."

"I gotta get back to the lights," I said as I saw Roman getting rid of his trash.

"And we have to go for a walk," Barbara said. She stacked up the table's trash and trays and took them away.

"After you do your thing are you going to stay around or head back to your place to rest?" I asked Nate.

"I'm gonna stay here, give support to everyone. Figure we can grab dinner as usual at the end of the day."

"Sounds good."

"To the stage?" Barbara asked, holding out a hand for Nate.

"Off we go." He grabbed the ice pack and his crutch as he stood. "To the stage." He leaned in and we shared a quick kiss. "See you later."

"See ya, Todd." Devin said before taking off after Barbara and Nate.

It was the first time I'd shared lunch with his friends. It felt comfortable. It felt good.

"Two minutes until we go," sounded the PA voice. I shook myself out of my thoughts and got a move on before Roman thought I'd deserted him.

TEN

I SPENT my first week back on vacation keeping busy with some projects around the house, reading, and sometimes just being lazy in the hammock. If Nate was free at night, we'd get together. As the show drew near the finale, he had more routines to learn each week. We both knew there'd be more time for us once the show was done in a couple of weeks. He kept a relentless pace, not letting the ankle injury slow him down one bit. Luckily he only iced it for three days before it felt good enough without it.

I was giddy to finally watch the show from the audience. To make it all the more exciting, I was in the VIP section, using one of Nate's passes. As I was waiting in line to enter the studio, Martin walked by.

He did a double-take as he saw me.

"You didn't just use your employee pass to go in?" His voice was the Martin I usually knew, not the angry one from our last encounter.

"Nah. I'm just a civilian today."

He lowered his voice and leaned in towards me. I stepped closer to the railings as well, so the rest of the line wouldn't necessarily hear whatever he was about to say.

"I'm sorry about the other day. I was outta line. I haven't had the balls to say that to you. Can we grab some coffee after the show, or tomorrow?"

"Of course." I was glad that he'd calmed down and, apparently, reconsidered. "Tomorrow's better. Nate doesn't have rehearsal right after the show, so we're having a quiet night."

"Tomorrow it is then. Let's have lunch. It'll have to be here, if that's okay."

"Perfect. Commissary never does me wrong. Twelve-thirty?"

He nodded. "I'll meet you at the door." He gestured to the line that was starting to move, right on time. "Enjoy the show."

"Oh, I will."

He clapped me on the back as I started to move.

Nate hadn't told me what he was working on this week. I knew he had the usual dance with Barbara, plus he'd be doing a number with Devin and two of the all-star guys as well as a solo. Now that I wasn't working the show anymore, I'd get to vote tonight and I was glad I could contribute to his total score. Voting was crucial since next week was the finale.

I sat where I'd be out of the range of the mounted cams. If someone wanted to put a picture of me on the screen, they were going to have to use one of the hand-helds, and that meant it probably wouldn't happen since it'd be more work.

A couple of twenty-something girls were on my left and no one was on my right since I was next to a stair-case. The girls were chattering and had signs for Devin. One of them turned to me as we got closer to showtime and decided to talk.

"You're the guy Nathaniel was out with, right?"

Oh, boy. We hadn't been back in the paper, but we knew that one set of pictures circulated widely and that I'd been identified. The show's PR department controlled who Nate talked to, and they were main-taining a no comment on competitors' private lives, which was always their stance. If these girls recognized me, someone else might, too.

"Yeah."

Again, truth seemed best.

"Cool. He's a cutie. You guys been going out long?"

At least for her it seemed like this was no big deal.

"Just a few weeks."

"Tell him we're his fans, too. We know Devin from school, but Nathaniel's pretty awesome."

I broke my reserve and smiled. "You might get to meet him afterwards, if you're hanging out with Devin. They're roommates, after all. I'm sure Devin would introduce you."

"Fun! I'm Natalie, by the way. This is Bella."

"Todd," I said, waving at Bella since she was further away.

"Two minutes to show," came a voice over the sound system. The audience cheered and the girls next to me squealed a little, too. I was excited and even had a nervous feeling in my stomach even though all I had to do was watch and enjoy. Seeing my favorite show live, and knowing my man was in it, was pretty freakin' cool.

At the countdown from thirty seconds, all the lights were set and the audience was asked to be quiet, but ready to applaud when the host was done with the intro.

On cue, the lights came up on Selena, the host, as she delivered her intro. "It's week nine and we've got your top four dancers performing with all-stars. These performances will determine who's in next week's finale. Welcome to *America's Next Top Dancer*." The audience delivered thunderous applause as the intro music played over the sound system and the opening credits showed on the studio's video screens.

Dancers hustled into their positions for the opening number. Even in silhouette it was easy for me to pick out Nate. As soon as the titles were done, the lights flashed in a multi-colored explosion and the dancers did one of the most intricate hip hop numbers I'd seen for a group. It was hot watching Nate show off his swagger.

Once they hit their final pose on stage, the music kicked up again and they retreated into the wings for their individual intros. The audience made it clear who the favorites were by their applause and screams, and I let my own scream go when Nate came forward for his moment in the spotlight.

Nate's first number with Barbara was about forty minutes into the program. It was hard to focus on the rehearsal package because he was on stage, shirtless, sprawled across a bed with Barbara perched on the headboard waiting to begin once the video was done. The number was outrageous. She was in his dreams, terrorizing him for being a cheater. It was an intense jazz number that showcased a different side of both of them. The crowd went nuts when they were done. Barbara was poised over Nate, catlike, ready to strike.

"That was his best yet," Natalie said to me during the commercial break.

"I think so, too. They really nailed it."

It was another twenty-five minutes before he was back with Devin and two of the all-stars. During the commercial break before their turn, the crew was hustling around the stage, lifting up sections and putting down grates with catch basins. As the rehearsal package played, the guys came out in black pants, no shirts and hats in hand. They took their positions and rain started to fall.

The host was in the audience to intro them, and the crowd went wild as the guys got wet. They danced a fusion of styles to a version of "Singing in the Rain" I'd never heard before. There was some Broadway, hip hop, jazz, and maybe a hint of paso doble. It was spectacular. I looked forward to watching it again at home because in the moment I could only watch Nate. He was breathtaking.

It was over too soon. The audience, once again, was in awe and many, including me, gave them a standing ovation, as did a couple of the judges.

As soon as the host had the dancers at her side for critiques, the stage crew was drying off the stage and getting the grates covered. Given the number of people, it looked like it might have been the entire backstage crew working on it. Selena was funny trying not to get her couture dress dripped on. The judges praised the group as well as the choreographer for what they called the dance of the night.

Nate was back right after the commercial, dried off and in jeans, a white t-shirt and black shoes for his thirty-second solo. Of course, I loved it. It was a contemporary dance done to music that featured a solo violinist. It had a poignant feel and I think he connected with every single person in the audience.

At the end of the evening, Selena recapped the dances and the ways to vote before signing off. As the general audience filed out, some dancers came into the VIP area to talk with their friends, while some of the other VIPs made their way up on stage. I stayed where I was. Nate and Devin had a lot of people around them and I didn't want to intrude.

"Can we really just go up there?" Natalie asked me after fidgeting in her seat for a couple of minutes.

"Absolutely."

She still looked hesitant.

"Come on," I said, standing up. I decided it was a different matter if I took them up rather than just going by myself.

I led them the long way around the front of the stage. They might know Devin, but it was clear they were big fans of the show just like I was. Going up the stage stairs that the host used, I distinctly heard a squeal from behind me and I had to contain a chuckle.

Devin had moved to a group with one of the judges, Selena, and a couple other audience members. Nate was across the stage. As I approached Devin's group, he caught sight of who was with me and ran up to the girls, arms open wide.

"You guys made it. I couldn't see you out there." They had a group hug. "Hey, Todd, good to see you, too. Enjoy the show from the audience?"

"Very much. Looking forward to tomorrow and next week, too."

"Todd, got a minute?" It was Clive calling me over from the wings. I nodded in his direction.

"I'll catch you guys later," I told the trio.

"Thanks for bringing us up," Bella said.

"You're welcome," I said, smiling at her. I crossed to Clive and Roman. "What's up, guys?"

"Any chance you can work the finale next week?" Clive asked.

That was a surprise. Since the guy I replaced was back, I hadn't expected to get recalled. Truth be told, I'd rather watch from the audience, but being on the crew again could lead to something more long-term with the show.

"Sure," I said before I could overthink it.

"Excellent. One less person we need to find." Clive indicated to follow him off stage. "It was decided today that we're going to do the finale outside. They haven't figured out where yet, but somewhere on the lot. It'll mean two to three times the audience, plus a ton of stage to build in the next week. The dancers will find out tomorrow, and it'll be announced on the show."

"Cool." I don't know if I was responding more as a tech or as a fan of the show.

"Can you start back tomorrow? I know that's super short notice, but you already know how we do things. We can get you on the team that's working on the finale straightaway. For the show, it'll be an hour on Tuesday for performance and then two hours Wednesday for season recap and the winner announcement. All on the outdoor stage."

"I'm in. Regular five-thirty call tomorrow?"

Clive thought about it. "Let me shoot you an email later this evening. I want to make sure we've got a plan before I have people show up."

"I'll keep an eye out for it. Thanks, Clive. Great to be back with you guys."

We shook hands. "We're glad to have you back."

He went off, no doubt to work on more of the new details.

"Excellent," Roman said. "I told him you'd come back."

"Of course. How can I say no to my favorite show?"

He smiled and clapped me on the back. "Get back out there and tell your guy how great he was tonight."

"Thanks, Roman."

Nate was with Devin, Bella, Natalie and some others. As I walked out of the wings, he saw me and ran across the stage. For a second I thought he was going to leap into my arms, but luckily he slowed up and just gave me a hug.

"You were incredible," I said, fighting the urge to run my hands over him. I whispered in his ear, "I'm thinking we may need to install a rain system in the bedroom so I can watch you do that again."

"Hmmmm. You're bad."

"Congrats on a great night," I said. "I see top three in your future."

"Shhhh," he whispered. "Don't jinx it. What were you talking about in the shadows?" He changed the subject so I couldn't put him at further risk.

I raised my eyebrows at him. "I can't tell you everything, except I'm back on the show. The reason is hush-hush until tomorrow."

"Oooh. Intrigue. I like it. And cool that you're back. I think." He paused a moment, keeping me in his embrace. "I'm not sure if I like it better with you in the audience or working somewhere nearby."

I laughed. "I thought about that, too. Being in the audience exceeded my expectations, and I'll still be there tomorrow. But I'm also excited to get back on the crew."

"Hey guys," Devin said coming over to us. "We're going to grab some dinner, do you want to come with? I hear Bella and Natalie made friends with Todd during the show already."

Nate looked at me and I nodded. I was okay hanging out for a while since I knew he was coming back to my place tonight.

ELEVEN

I was at Bar Three-Two when I got a text from Nate. The group rehearsal ended earlier than expected and he was checking to see if I was still hanging out with some of the crew.

Roman talked me into joining him and some of the others when we'd wrapped for the day. It was a bonus that Paul, one of my best friends from *Dealmakers*, happened to be here, too.

I quickly texted back: *I'm still here. You can come if you want, or I can meet you somewhere.*

Nate wasted no time replying: *I'll be there in a few.*

I texted him the address and he replied that he was on his way.

"What's got you grinning?" asked Paul.

"Nate's on his way over."

"No way! I finally get to meet him?"

"Yup. He got done early."

We'd been planning to throw a small barbecue at

my house after *ANTD* wrapped so Nate could meet my friends. I was glad he'd get to meet Paul sooner.

Paul, Roman and I were talking about various mishaps we'd all been through doing shows. Roman had the best stories as he'd done live TV for years. He'd done a couple seasons on a talent competition and was telling a story about the smackdown that happened between a singer and a dancer who were using the same song.

"The performers weren't having it," Roman explained. "The dancer slugged the singer and broke his nose two minutes before the he was due to go on. Neither of them got on the air because the singer was bleeding and the dancer was arrested. We had eight minutes to fill with only thirty to go. Those poor judges had to stretch their critiques so far. It was hilarious every time we went to commercial as the crew listened to the director scramble."

As we laughed, arms slipped around my waist and someone pressed up against my back.

"Hey, Sexy Big Man," Nate whispered in my ear. "What's so funny?"

I took one of his hands and pulled him around next to me so I could give him a proper kiss. He was in blue jeans, dark sneakers and black t-shirt. It was his standard casual outfit, but the way the jeans hugged his butt and the shirt hung off his lean shoulders always piqued my interest.

"Good to see you. You guys finished way early."

"Yeah," he said, something between weariness and

irritation in his voice. "There was a bit of a meltdown between the choreographer and Daniele. It wasn't pretty and that ended the day. Barbara was already exhausted, so she and I decided to get together early tomorrow to work on our stuff. It'll be interesting to see what ends up on TV because the cameras were there for all of it."

"Oh, man. That sounds bad. They don't usually show confrontation, though."

Nate nodded. "Yeah. Hopefully they don't. Neither one of them will end up in a good light. Professionalism went right out the window."

"You must be Nate," Paul said, introducing himself. "I've heard a lot about you."

Nate smiled as he shook Paul's hand. "Todd's told me some great stories about you two." Nate winked at me. I'd told him about a few of our attempts at being wingman for each other.

"And you're still talking to me, that's good." Paul smirked. "I can only imagine what he's told you about some of our misadventures. I'm glad to see he does better when I'm not around."

Nate fit in so easily. It was like he'd been friends with Paul forever. He and Paul shared a love of the Florida Panthers that I could never have predicted.

"I'll check the schedule," Paul said. "Florida will get here once. If you're in town we should all go, or we could catch another game. I usually go a few times a season."

I rolled my eyes. I didn't get hockey. Paul tried to educate me a couple years ago, and I was bored silly.

"You don't like it?" Nate asked, sounding horrified. "Best sport ever. Fast, a little violent, what's not to like?"

"Maybe he'll like it better if you're there," Paul offered.

"I'll give it another shot," I said. "If you both like it, there's got to be something I just haven't caught onto yet."

"Deal!" Paul said.

A shriek sounded from the other side of the bar. A woman was quickly coming our way, waving her arms in the air.

"Oh my God, I love you on *Dancer* so much." The woman ignored everyone else while she stood directly in front of Nate, talking too loud.

"Thanks," Nate said, just as smooth as if he were meeting someone who hadn't just acted like a crazy person.

This was the first time I'd witnessed Nate getting called out by a fan in public. Luckily he didn't seem to mind. I slipped an arm around his waist, just to make it clear he was mine.

"Would you dance for me? Right now?" she asked brazenly. "That'd be so amazing. A perfect birthday present."

Nate looked at me and I shrugged. "It's up to you," I said.

He gave me a smile and raised his eyebrows. He had a plan.

"For the birthday girl," he said and the woman squealed.

He looked around, and when he spotted the sound system behind the bar he took off, but not before giving my hand a squeeze. Nate talked with one of the bartenders. They seemed to be flipping pages on a tablet. Finally, Nate pointed and nodded.

Christina Aguilera's "Show Me How You Burlesque" came on, much louder than what had been playing. Nate sat on a bar stool during Christina's a cappella intro. He was leaning back against the bar, looking very cool. When the music kicked in, he jumped from the seat up onto the bar and started doing some intricate moves. The crowd clapped in time to the music.

It was a sexy number. He knew the song well, so his musicality was perfect. During the chorus he motioned for people to give him room, which he used to jump off the bar. He danced his way over to us and held a hand out for the birthday girl. She shrieked again before taking his hand.

For the last half of the song, Nate led her through a myriad of moves while the crowd cheered. When the song ended, the music went back to the normal mix and volume and Nate bowed to his dance partner, who looked a little flustered. They came back to our group.

"That was amazing," she said, sounding out of

breath. "Thank you. That was a helluva birthday present." She was beaming.

"My pleasure." Nate seemed to really enjoy that. "It was fun. I've wanted to dance to that on the show, but they can't get the rights for the song. So I'm glad I got to do it somewhere. If you'll excuse me, I'm going to get something to drink."

"Thanks, again," she said before leaving us.

"That was really nice of you," Paul said when Nate returned.

"It was cool, although it would've been better dancing it with you." He gave me a quick kiss before he drank down half a bottle of water. "How was lunch? I didn't get to ask you earlier."

"Surprisingly good. We made up. I even invited Martin to the barbecue."

"What was the problem anyway?

"He hooked up with a contestant on some castaway show a few years back. She said she was totally into him, turned out she was sleeping with several guys on the crew. She got caught, everyone got exposed, he lost his job. He was half looking out for me and half jealous that I'd found someone on the show."

"Wow. I'm glad we're not that complicated."

"Me, too."

We hung out with Paul and Roman for another half-hour before we called it a night and headed back to my place.

TWELVE

THE SEVEN DAYS leading up to the finale were insane. Rigging the stage that was fifty percent bigger than the usual one, plus installing the judges' desk from the main set and an array of video monitors for the audience was a lot of work to complete in a short time. I had a new appreciation for outdoor live television event set-up, which is something I hadn't done before.

Nate and I stole moments at lunch to say hello and we slept together a couple of nights. It was just sleep. We were both exhausted. With the competition in its final week, Nate had more than ever to learn with three new dances and four others to brush up on.

The stage was spectacular, and it was exciting to watch the dancers work on it during dress rehearsals. The designers did a great job on the lighting elements. Since we'd be live at five o'clock both nights, they put the stage in a spot where it would be in shadow, rather than direct sun, so there'd be a mix of natural and stage light.

For Tuesday's show, I was stuck behind the stage working on a myriad of tasks. Nate made it into the final three and knew he'd be performing a lot Wednesday, including a number he had to learn overnight with the two girls who made it through. We had about ten minutes together after the show before he headed off to rehearsal.

The great thing was that we both knew we'd go home together Wednesday because the show would be over.

The Wednesday night finale was incredible. Part of me yearned to be in the audience. The energy coming off them, even an hour ahead of the show, was insane. Dancers from past seasons were performing some classic routines. These were being streamed on the show's website, so it was essentially another complete show happening before the finale.

Once the pre-show was done, I set up what I needed to for the start of the big show and went to find Nate. He was in the makeshift backstage area, made mostly out of curtains, doing some last-minute rehearsing with Barbara. All around, dancers and crew were bustling to get things ready.

"Sorry to interrupt," I said as he was putting her down from a lift.

"Hey, stranger." Nate said, grinning.

I heard the exhaustion in his voice, despite the

huge smile he displayed. I couldn't imagine how hard he'd been pushing his body the past few days.

"I'll let you two have a moment. It's a good excuse for me to go sit down for a second." Barbara smiled wearily, grabbing her water bottle and heading for a nearby empty chair.

"Just wanted to wish you a good show," I said, wrapping him in my arms. Heat radiated off him as he stood before me in tight black pants and a black tank top.

"Thanks." Despite his tiredness there was a spark in his eyes that told me he was fired up. "Where are you going to be stationed tonight?"

"All over the place," I said. "I'm in a different spot for almost every number because there's so much going on."

It was true, with the countdown of the season's top numbers, we couldn't always do pre-sets in the best way. It was going to be an epic show, but not the easiest to pull off.

He nodded. "Maybe we'll just watch it at home tonight, since I won't get to see any of it either. I think I'll just be getting ready for one thing after the other."

"We can do whatever you want after."

We smiled and I gave him a big hug and kiss.

"Hmmmm. I love being wrapped up in my sexy big man."

"Five minutes to live. That's five minutes, every-one." The voice over the PA sent the audience into hysterics and the crew into a renewed hustle.

"Love you," I said.

"Love you, too. I'll see you after."

I'D NEVER WORKED AS HARD as I did on the finale. It was exhilarating. The crew had its own choreography, making sure it all flowed seamlessly.

I kept up with what was being said on stage, even when I wasn't able to see it. With twenty minutes left in the show it was Nate and Barbara in the top two. I applauded for a moment at the announcement. During the commercial break that followed, I powered down what I'd just operated and was about to climb up to the light grid.

"Clive for Todd. Need you down front, stage left."

I hung on to the ladder with one hand as I got on the radio. "Todd for Clive. Confirm the change, please. I'm scheduled for the grid."

"Clive for Todd. Confirmed."

I hustled to get to the new location, which involved going through a maze of curtains since I couldn't cut across the stage. I was there with less than thirty seconds until the show was back. Clive was there, which was strange since I imagined he had about a million things to do.

"Your job for the next six minutes is to be right here," Clive said, patting the railing at the side of the bleacher seating. "Just watch. You'll move to your next position as soon as Selena introduces the video package." He pulled a folded paper from his pocket and smiled as he handed it to me "This is from Nate." He was gone before I could say anything.

I opened it and recognized Nate's scrawled handwriting. *This performance is dedicated to my sexy big man. I'm glad I get to do this again since it's the dance that really started our thing. Love you, N.*

I wished I had some Kleenex because I knew what was scheduled next. Nate and Barbara, along with the host, took to the stage seconds before the commercial break ended. The show came back with a video package showing Barbara and Nate through various rehearsals and performances before cutting to Selena for the introduction.

"And now with the number one dance you wanted to see again, with their Viennese waltz from week four, it's Barbara and Nathaniel."

The dance was beautiful, even more so than the first time. It had become our dance. I was better at doing it now because Nate had kept working with me. We weren't going to dance it at the wrap party tonight, because that terrified me. But I looked forward to working on it more with him, and maybe I'd do it in public one day.

After the dance, Nate bowed in my direction. Many people were obviously in on making it so I could see this performance from the audience. Between the beauty of the dance and the thoughtfulness of the crew I worked with, I was overcome with emotion.

Once the next video package started, I darted to

my next position, which was to bring on stage and connect a set piece that would be used for the final group number. It was the last thing to happen before the winner was announced. I got that set just as the group was getting into place. I had no idea how Nate and Barbara quick changed like that, but they made it right on time.

All of the contestants were together for the first time in weeks, with Nate and Barbara front and center. I got to watch this high energy number from just off stage and I sort of bounced along with the beat. As the dance drew to a close, dancers left the stage, in the order they'd been eliminated, until it was just Nate and Barbara striking the final pose.

"It's down to Barbara and Nathaniel," Selena said as she joined them on stage. "One of them is about to be crowned America's Next Top Dancer. All will be revealed, after the break."

During the commercial, Nate and Barbara darted off for another quick change while I helped clear the stage. As I exited, Nate and I came face-to-face. He was the epitome of handsome in a perfectly fitted black suit. We stared at each other until the thirty second call came over the PA. I took his hand, gave it a quick kiss and he winked at me. Barbara darted past us in a sparkly silver dress and Nate took off right behind her to take their positions next to Selena.

"After ten weeks of competition," Selena said, on cue. "it's come down to this."

I headed up to the grid as she spoke. I didn't have

much to do there, except to watch over things for safety since all kinds of lights were going to flash and fireworks were going to shoot off from above the stage.

"The vote was the closest it's ever been. With millions of votes cast, the final tally has a separation of just over five hundred votes. Are you ready?" Selena looked out to the audience and they went wild, waving signs for either Nate or Barbara. She then looked to Nate and Barbara. "Ready?"

They nodded and Barbara took Nate's hand.

"Okay, here we go." The lights flashed bright before the stage darkened, leaving only Selena, Barbara and Nate in white light. Dramatic music kicked in. Selena opened the seal on the card she held. "After ten weeks of competition, the viewers have voted and America's Next Top Dancer is..."

I CLICKED OFF THE TV. Nate and I were curled up on the couch and the show had just finished. We'd watched it, from the top, when we got home from the after party.

"You're probably one of the most gracious runners-up I've ever seen on the show," I said, giving him a hug.

"Barbara totally deserved it. The solo she did last night alone was worthy of the win." I completely disagreed, but I wasn't going to debate it. "Besides, with that narrow margin in the votes, it's hard to consider it a loss."

I untangled myself from him and stood up.

"Where're you going?"

"Just hang tight one second." I scampered off to the bedroom to get the surprise I had for him. I kept it behind my back as I returned. "Nathaniel Mayer," I said, using my best announcer's voice, "you may be the runner up for *America's Next Top Dancer*, but you're officially Sexy Big Man's Top Dancer."

I revealed a trophy, which was cheap—gold plated and fake marble. The figure on top was a dancer with a leg and arm extended. I had it engraved with Nate's name, along with the title I'd given him.

The smile was huge as he jumped off the couch and took the trophy from me.

"Oh my God, this is amazing." He calmed himself quickly and stood holding it as if he were on camera. "This is the highest honor I could've received. I promise to live up to this title each and every day. Thank you so much."

He bowed a couple of times before throwing a big hug around me.

"I'm so proud of you." I kissed him. "Was it fun doing all that tonight?"

"Yeah. But it all went by so fast. I wish I could've slowed it down. All those people screaming was pretty unreal. I'm glad we just watched it while it's fresh in my mind." He put the trophy on top of the TV. "I'll leave this right here so you'll remember me while I'm on tour."

"I seriously doubt I could forget you."

He yawned and I grabbed his hand, taking him back to the bedroom.

"Is it okay if I sleep for about three days?" he asked.

"Only if I get to stay in bed with you."

"I wouldn't have it any other way."

We kissed at the foot of the bed as we got out of our clothes.

"What time do we have to get your stuff out of the apartment?" I asked, taking a break in the kisses.

"Aw, man." He frowned. "It's between nine and noon. So much for three days in bed."

"Nah, we'll be back in no time. Then we can make out, fall asleep, eat and do it all over again until you start rehearsals and I go back to work."

"Mmmmmm." He nuzzled into my chest. "It's going to be awesome if you get to come on tour."

"Yeah. Hopefully the show's recommendation will give me an advantage."

I had an interview with the tour company at the end of next week. I was trying not to set my expectations too high, but I thought I had a decent chance at snagging a job. We finally lay down in bed and got into our usual positions where I was partially on top of him.

"What if you get sick of me, spending so much time together?"

"I don't think that's possible," I said. "If anything the past few weeks have shown me that I only want more time."

He intertwined his fingers in mine. "Good." He smiled a very sleepy smile.

He snuggled closer and his breathing shifted in no time. After the craziness of the last few days, it wasn't surprising he drifted off so fast. With the end of the show, we were moving into a new phase of our relationship. I was excited to see where we were headed next.

AUTHOR'S NOTE

I've had a great time revisiting this story and fleshing out Todd and Nate's relationship further. The original story, *Dancer and Sexy Big Man*, was written to meet a specific word count. With it twice as long now, you get more details on how Todd and Nate became a couple. I'm thrilled to bring this story back. It's always been a favorite since I love dance competition shows as much as I love hockey.

Thanks to my wonderful husband, Will Knauss, for all his support and reading. Thanks also to Michael Spires for his reading and line editing.

ALSO BY JEFF ADAMS

Hockey Romance

Head in the Game

The Hockey Player's Heart (co-written with Will Knauss)

The Hockey Player's Snow Day

Keeping Kyle (A Hockey Allies Bachelor Bid Romance)

Rivals

On Stage Series

Dancing for Him

Love's Opening Night

More Romance Titles

A Sound Beginning

Room Service

Somewhere on Mackinac

Summer Heat

Young Adult Titles

Each of these are available in ebook, paperback and
audiobook

Codename: Winger series

Tracker Hacker (includes the bonus short story *A Very Winger Christmas*)

Schooled

Audio Assault

Netminder

Other Young Adult Titles

Flipping for Him

ABOUT THE AUTHOR

Jeff Adams has written stories since he was in middle school and became a published author in 2009 when his first short stories were published. He writes both gay romance and LGBTQ young adult fiction...and there's usually a hockey player at the center of the story.

Jeff lives in central California with his husband of more than twenty years, Will. Some of his favorite things include the musicals *Rent* and [*title of show*], the Detroit Red Wings and Pittsburgh Penguins hockey teams, and the reality TV competition *So You Think You Can Dance*. He, of course, loves to read, but there isn't enough space to list out his favorite books.

Jeff and Will are also podcasters. The *Big Gay Fiction Podcast* is a weekly show devoted to gay romance as well as pop culture. New episodes come out every Monday at BigGayFictionPodcast.com.

Learn more about Jeff, his books and find his social media links at JeffAdamsWrites.com. From the website you can also sign up for his newsletter to get a free ebook of *The Hockey Player's Snow Day*, as well serialized stories, previews of new books, book recommendations and more!